William Horsell

The Vegetarian armed at all Points

Anatiposi

William Horsell

The Vegetarian armed at all Points

Reprint of the original.

1st Edition 2023 | ISBN: 978-3-38230-554-3

Anatiposi Verlag is an imprint of Outlook Verlagsgesellschaft mbH.

Verlag (Publisher): Outlook Verlag GmbH, Zeilweg 44, 60439 Frankfurt, Deutschland
Vertretungsberechtigt (Authorized to represent): E. Roepke, Zeilweg 44, 60439 Frankfurt, Deutschland
Druck (Print): Books on Demand GmbH, In de Tarpen 42, 22848 Norderstedt, Deutschland

THE VEGETARIAN

ARMED AT ALL POINTS:

IN WHICH THE

THEORY IS EXPLAINED;

THE

CHIEF ARGUMENTS ADVANCED;

AND THE

PRINCIPAL OBJECTIONS ANSWERED.

BY WILLIAM HORSELL,

Author of "Hydropathy for the People," etc.

London:

VEGETARIAN DEPOT, 492, OXFORD STREET.
And Sold by all Booksellers.

PREFACE.

It is not surprising that an organization, embracing all the laws of hygiene, including the facts, Anatomy, Chemistry, Physiology, History, &c., as the Vegetarian Society does, should be beset with many difficulties, ignorance being the chief. This being the case, the author conceived the idea of executing such a pamphlet as is now before the reader. He has done what he could, he is happy to say, with the cordial approbation of several warm friends of the cause to whom the work was submitted in manuscript, and each of whom he desires to thank for valuable emendations and corrections.

The author's object has been to furnish such a compendium of the theory and principles of Vegetarianism, as would come within the means of most persons to purchase, distribute, read, and understand ; and as he has not sought originality, he has taken advantage of all available sources for facts and illustrations. Sometimes he has given the sentiments, at other times the words of the authors he has consulted, but has generally preferred to omit quotations, in order that the mind of the reader should not be distracted from his subject. He thinks it right to say he has consulted and quoted the following works, which he strongly recommends to those who desire to be more fully informed. He has placed them in the order in which he esteems them. *The Science of Human Life; The Philosophy of Sacred History; Fruits and Farinacea the proper Food for Man; Vegetable Diet; The Hydropathic Encyclopedia; Anthropology, or the Science of Human Nature;* and *The Vegetarian Messenger.*

INTRODUCTION.

PARTICULAR periods of the world's history appear to have been especially devoted to the development of certain grand principles; the most prominent question of *this* being *Social Reform*. Certain individuals have also been raised up and qualified by Divine Providence for the execution of His purposes, though their labors do not appear to have been fully appreciated by their contemporaries, or to have been crowned with success in their own day.

LINNÆUS and his *labors* were of this class. He was a diligent student of nature; a clear and original thinker; and did, perhaps, more to give succeeding generations correct and exalted views of the character and goodness of God, as exhibited in the kingdom of nature, than any other man; and that chiefly by the method and order of his arrangement. To his sagacious discernment science is indebted for the division of plants, of animals, of herbs, &c., into classes.

Free agency, and consequent responsibility for all his actions, is the grand characteristic difference between man and the lower orders of creation. By this principle only can we have any test of his obedience to the physical, mental, and moral laws; and by the results of our actions in each sphere we are enabled to judge of the actions themselves. It follows from these premises that bodily health and vigour, and the consequent proper action of the whole frame, can only be attained by compliance with the physical laws of our being: nor has the Creator left us without the means of judging, but has provided a clear line of demarcation between the good and the bad; so that man, looking at the nature and effects of the various habits of life, and of substances used as food, or otherwise, should be enabled to live in such a manner as would promote the best and highest conditi on of his whole being.

LINNÆUS has rendered us efficie nt aid in this respect. By withdrawing the veil which had obscured the beauties and bounties of nature, he displayed them to the world;

and thus by taking *cause* and *effect* for his guide, he has raised a rampart of truth around the animal, vegetable, and mineral kingdoms, which neither interest nor malice can destroy. The Bible, Linnæus, experience, science, and facts, rightly understood, all harmonise and exhibit such wisdom and goodness in the works of God, as must convince every *honest* mind, that His purposes and plans can only result in unmixed good to His creatures, unless their blindness and perverseness interfere to prevent it. We recommend the study of Linnæus. "Method," he remarks, "the soul of science, indicates that every natural body may by inspection be known by its own peculiar name or nature;" that "the study of natural history consists in the collection, arrangement, and exhibition of the various productions of the earth." Let us apply these ideas to our present purposes.

The universe comprehends whatever exists—whatever can come to our knowledge by the agencies of our senses; such as the stars, the elements, and the earth.

The earth and its productions are divided by Linnæus into the three grand kingdoms of *Animals, Vegetables,* and *Minerals;* the boundaries of the former meet in the Zoophytes. Of these three grand divisions, the animal kingdom ranks highest in comparative estimation, next the vegetable, and last and lowest the mineral.

Minerals exist in the interior of the earth, in rude and shapeless masses, are generated by salts, and are without life or sensation.

Vegetables clothe the surface of the earth with food and verdure; inspire their nourishment, chiefly during the day, from the poisonous or carbonaceous parts of the atmosphere, and respire oxygen, or the healthy parts of the atmosphere, thus preserving it pure for the purposes of the animal kingdom. Vegetables are organised bodies, having life, but not sensation.

Animals adorn the exterior of the earth; are organised bodies, having life, sensation, and the power of locomotion.

Man, the last and best of created works, formed after "the image of God," endowed with high intellectual and moral powers, the lord and subjugator of all other animals, is, by his wisdom, judgment, and free agency, alone capable of examining, judging, and determining on the propriety of his physical, intellectual, and moral conduct, and therefore a fit subject for rewards and punishments. Hence the object of every person should be, first, to study the nature of his own organisation, and the nature and effects of the bodies, elements, and influence which constitute the food, drink, clothing, air, &c., on that organisation. This view cannot, perhaps, be better expressed than in the language of Mr. Combe, who says: "The first object of mankind, as intellectual beings in quest of happiness, must be to study the elementary qualities of their own being, and their applications, and the relationship between these. His second object will be to discover, and carry into effect, the conditions—physical, intellectual, and moral—which, in virtue of this constitution, require to be realized before the fullest enjoyment of which they. are capable can be attained.

These views have the entire sympathy of that class of Dietetic Reformers, called Vegetarians ; whose object in their various organisations is to spread them as rapidly and extensively as possible. Believing that an amazing amount of ignorance exists on these matters, resulting iu crime and misery, which *can*, and therefore *ought* to be removed, they think they are discharging a high moral duty to the community and posterity, as well as manifesting their gratitude to the Giver of all Good, for the advantages they have derived from the adoption of a "bloodless diet," and the observance of other organic laws. So strongly are many of them impressed with these views that they thiuk they could not honorably acquit themselves before God or man if they held their "peace at *such* a time," on such a subject. They regard themselves similarly situated with the four leprous men at the entering in of the gate of Samaria, at the time of the siege and *famine*, who having discovered that the affrighted Syrians had fled, and left abundance of provisions in their tents, while the people of the city were starving of hunger, they exclaimed, " We do not well. This is a day of good tidings, and we hold our peace : if we tarry till the morning light, some mischief will come upon us ; now therefore, come, that we may go and tell the king's household."

And now, reader, what have we to tell you ? Hearken !

We believe living on the Vegetarian principle is not only more economical, but a much healthier and happier mode of existence ; and therefore we wish to call your serious attention to the facts and reasonings which are here set before you. Let it be distinctly understood, *we have no quarrel with you*. If, after a careful examination and a *fair trial*, you still think it best to slaughter and devour animals, you are, doubtless, *permitted* to do so. But our object is to show you a more excellent way.

CHAPTER I.

THE THEORY OF VEGETARIANISM.

SOME persons have taken strong objections to the term *Vegetarianism;* but as we are not aware of their having given us the choice of a better, we prefer to retain the original. Vegetarianism is derived from *vegeto,* which might also be from the Latin *vegeto,* and that again from the Greek ενεχην, which, in English, means *"to be in vigour; to come to the perfection of vigour or strength; to be sound and whole; to grow, to move."* Vegetarianism is the art or science which teaches man to "cull, dispose, and modify for food those productions of the vegetable kingdom only, which are best adapted to produce and sustain a sound mind, in a sound body." The word Vegetarian itself is almost convincing: all the ancient physiologists thought that *vegetus* was the most proper word to convince their fellow-men that their physical proportions could be best developed and best supported by a *"growing diet,'* a *"strong diet,"* a *"fresh, lively, gallant food* or diet ;" for the word *vegetable* has all those meanings, and many more in ordinary language. It is a science that teaches men how to live without *doctors* or physicians, that is, such doctors and physicians as apply and prescribe *medicines* for the cure of diseases ; it teaches man how to avoid diseases by living according to the laws of nature and of nature's God ; it is the art of preserving animal life, and not of destroying it.

Vegetarianism, in its most simple acceptance, means abstinence from the flesh of animals as food ; in a more extended sense, it comprises all the religious and moral duties of man in his intercourse with his fellow-creatures. There are various motives which influence man in the adoption of this system. Some are actuated chiefly by the conviction that the infliction of pain upon the lower animals and the taking away animal life, are infringements of the great laws of moral duty, and that there is no reason why the command, "Thou shalt not *kill*," should not have respect to the lower animals as well as to man : others are chiefly influenced by the fact, that the practice of Vegerarian habits conduces to a higher and more perfect development of the physical powers and mental perceptions, and tends to the promotion of health and to the attainment of longevity ; and others, again, by motives of economy and independence in worldly matters. But all are unanimous in the conviction, that the natural diet of man is one consisting of fruits and farinaceous substances, and that the strength and agility of the frame, the preservation of health, the growth of intellectual power and moral feeling, together with a higher enjoyment of life, are to be obtained only by the adoption of the Vegetarian practice.

By ¡Vegetarianism, we do not imply a *mere* system of abstinence from eating the flesh of animals, for such a system has always been the practice of a vast majority of the human race; but, by Vegetarianism, we mean that system which has been adopted by prophets and philosophers, at different periods of the world, as calculated to increase the freedom and consequent power of the intellectual and moral faculties; to prepare the mind to withstand temptations to immorality and crime; a system, *adherence* to which, whatever may have been the first motive for its adoption, involves a desire to rise above sensuality in the scale of existence; to be devoted more and more to the cultivation and growth of the mind; which teaches us to abstain from flesh, because flesh-eating is a sensual indulgence, a carnivorous, an unclean thing; because it is cruel to kill, opposed to true civilisation, to justice, to mercy, to kindness, and to all those finer and nobler feelings which form the brightest ornaments to human character. It is the Vegetarianism of the *mind* as well as of the *body*. It is the Vegetarianism of Daniel the prophet when he wished his companions to be fair, comely, and wise. It is the Vegetarianism of Pythagoras, of Numa, of Plato, of Plutarch, of Franklin, of Swedenborg, of Newton, of Wesley, of Howard, and of such minds as these, whose lives are still held up as an example to our youth, and whose works form the foundation of much of the intellectual and moral education of the present day, and who are, in fact the *educators* of civilized society.— *Vegetarian Advocate*, p. 1, vol. i.

Hence, the great question of education—a question which is decidedly occupying a large share of public attention—is involved in this theory—*the education of life;* that which begins with the first smile of infancy, and we dare not say, ends with life itself. It comprehends the training of the *feelings* as well as the cultivation of the *intellect;* the practice of *morality*, as well as the practice of *mathematics;* the management of the *will*, as well as the development of the *understanding*. This is an education which affects our fire-sides and our dinner-tables;

our kitchens and our drawing-rooms ; our morning walks and our social *soirées ;* our private and our public intercourse with the world ; and, above all, it is an education which seems to affect our position in the scale of creation, whether *carnivorous, omnivorous,* or *herbivorous;* whether *clean* or *unclean, sensual* or *spiritual;* and, consequently, to affect our position in relation to the Creator himself !

Thus you will perceive that the term *Vegetarianism* involves something more than the mere eating or not eating certain substances. It embraces the why and the wherefore of doing or not doing so. The reign of PRINCE PALATE —who has neither eyes to see, nor ears to hear the truth— is at an end with the intelligent Vegetarian. Old CUSTOM with him is dead and buried. Show him that you are *right*, and he will follow you, but not else. Vegetarianism, therefore, involves the study of at least the general outline of anatomy, chemistry, physiology, history, medicine, politics, economics, experience, and intellectual and moral philosophy ; and no one can fully enter into the question of Vegetarianism unless he has turned his attention, to some extent, to these various branches of science.

Our theory therefore is, that the corn and fruits of the earth are man's *natural* and *best* food—that which was originally *appointed* for him by unerring Wisdom and Goodness in his unfallen state ; and that which was chiefly used by him during the early period of his history. We regard it as the true theory of dietetics established in his natural constitution ; and that as a physical, intellectual, and moral being (other things being equal), he can become most completely developed in all his faculties and functions by strictly adhering to the practice. All who carry out this principle, abstaining entirely " from the flesh of animals as food," are considered *Vegetarians*, and after one month's practice are eligible as members of the VEGETARIAN SOCIETY.

It is not our design to give an elaborate essay on each of the following topics, but an outline, and to consider them separately in relation to this great question of Dietetic Reform, referring our reader for further information to the standard works of Graham, Lamb, Alcott, Smith, and Trall ; but more especially to Graham's *Science of Human Life;* his *Philosophy of Sacred History ;* and Smith's *Fruits and Farinacea* the Proper Food of Man : works that have never yet been answered, and which we believe to be UN-ANSWERABLE.

CHAPTER II.

COMPARATIVE ANATOMY.

ANATOMY is the science of the structure of an organized body. An organized body consists of an assemblage of parts, each of which is called an organ, and all mutually related to, and dependent on, each other. All organized bodies are either animal or vegetable. Comparative Human Anatomy contemplates a knowledge and comparison of the structure of other animals, the structure of their several organs, and their relation to each other.

This is the stronghold of the advocates of flesh-eating, from which they think none can draw or drive them; whereas it is the weakest point of the position, and the key to the citadel. True, there are not wanting men of learning and science who seek to defend it, such as the MESSRS. CHAMBERS, DR. WILKINSON, and other moderns; and who assert that "Experienced naturalists, anatomists, and physiologists, reasoning from the structure of the teeth and intestinal canal, are confident that the human being is omnivorous;" feeding partly on roots and grain, and partly on flesh. Granted! if this is to be shewn by his daily *habits*. But the point is, *not* what man *is*, but what he *ought to be:* not what he *can* feed on, but what is *best* for him: what he is by *nature:* not what he is by *habit*: for these very gentlemen admit that many habits are not only unnatural, but wicked. It is also rather remarkable, that while these gentlemen make such assertions with great confidence, they never condescend to give us their authorities. We ask, therefore, who are the eminent anatomists and physiologists who support their views? and where shall we find their opinions and reasons recorded? We have "declared war," and set the battle in array against the theory and practice of flesh-eating, and we demand a manly defence, or a "surrender at discretion!"

Natural history alone solves the problem beyond all controversy as to what are man's *natural* dietetic habits; and although we think *reason* and *facts* are far superior to *authority*, the public generally do not, and therefore we meet them on their own ground. What says authority? All the most eminent naturalists and anatomists, as far as we know, are unanimous and positive in the opinion that the anatomical structure of the human body, as compared with other animals, places man with the frugivorous, and not with the omnivorous animals. We quote the following. LINNÆUS, of whom we have previously spoken, and who was one of the most celebrated naturalists that ever lived, speaking of fruits, says :—

" This species of food is that which is most suitable to man ; which is evinced by the series of quadrupeds, analogy, wild men, the structure of the mouth, of the stomach, and the hands." M. DAUBENTON, the associate of Buffon, observes : ' It is, then, highly probable that man, in a state of pure nature, living in a confined society, and in a genial climate, where the earth required but little culture to produce its fruits, did subsist upon these, without seeking to prey upon animals.'—GASSENDI, in his celebrated letter to Van Helmont, says : ' Wherefore I repeat, that from the primeval and spotless institution of our nature, the teeth were destined to the mastication, not of flesh, but of fruits.'—SIR EVERED HOME says : ' While mankind remained in a state of innocence, there is ground to believe that their only food was the produce of the vegetable kingdom.'—BARON CUVIER, whose knowledge of comparative anatomy was profound, and whose opinion, therefore, is entitled to the greatest respect, thus writes : ' Fruits, roots, and the succulent parts of vegetables, appear to be the natural food of man : his hands afford him a facility in gathering them ; and *his short and canine teeth, not passing beyond the common line of the others,* and the tubercular teeth, would not permit him either to feed on herbage, or devour flesh, unless these aliments were previously prepared by the culinary process.'—RAY, the celebrated botanist, asserts : ' Certainly, man by nature was never made to be a carnivorous animal, nor is he armed at all for prey or rapine, with jagged and pointed teeth, and crooked claws, sharpened to rend and tear ; but with gentle hands, to gather fruits and vegetables, and with teeth to chew and eat them.'—PROFESSOR LAWRENCE observes : ' The teeth of man have not the slightest resemblance to those of carnivorous animals, except that their enamel is confined to their external surface. He possesses, indeed, teeth called canine, but they do not exceed the level of the others, and are obviously unsuited to the purposes which the corresponding teeth execute in carnivorous animals.' * * ' Thus we find, that whether we consider the teeth and jaws, or the immediate

instruments of digestion, the human structure closely resembles that of the simiæ (or monkey tribe), all of which,
as we think everybody should know, in their natural

Fig. 1.

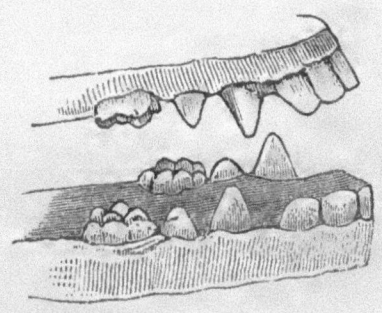

Jaw of the Infant Ourang-Outang.

state, are completely frugivorous.' (Fig. 1.)—LORD MON-
BODDO says: 'Though I think that man has, from nature,
the capacity of living either by prey or upon the fruits of
the earth, it appears to me, that by nature, and in his original state, he is a frugivorous animal, and that he only
becomes an animal of prey by acquired habit.'—MR.
THOMAS BELL observes: 'The opinion which I venture to
give has not been hastily formed, nor without what appear to me sufficient grounds. It is, I think, not going
too far to say, that every fact connected with the human
organization goes to prove that man was originally formed
a frugivorous animal, and therefore tropical, or nearly so,
with regard to his geographical position. This opinion is
principally derived from the formation of his teeth and
digestive organs, as well as from the character of his skin,
and the general structure of his limbs.'

DR. W. LAMBE, after a critical examination of the subject, says, "man is herbivorous in his structure," and his
conclusion was verified by more than forty years' vegetarian practice. DR. SYLVESTER GRAHAM, of America, who
with a mind singularly constituted to grasp first principles,
devoted forty years of his life to the study and minute
investigation of the whole question, with a zeal surpassing
that of any other man, confirms and illustrates the views
of all the other great authorities above quoted, in his hith-
erto unanswered works on *the Science of Human Life*, and
the Philosophy of Sacred History.

The incisors or cutting teeth of man, (*i.* Fig. 2.) are eight in number, large, broad, and compressed, with a flat

Fig. 2.

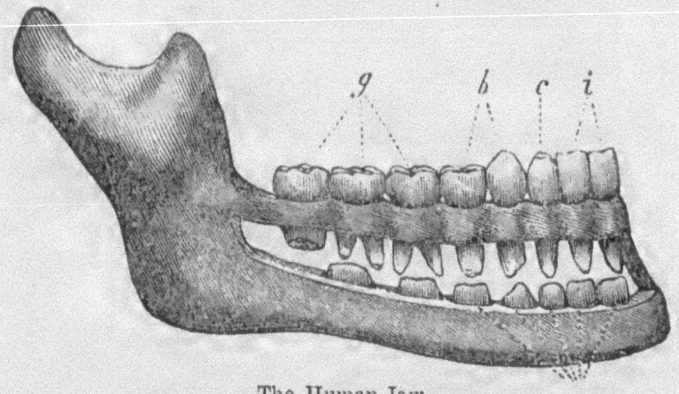

The Human Jaw

g, molars ; *b*, bicuspids ; *c*, cuspids ; *i*, incisors.

edge ; whilst those of the carnivorous animal are twelve in number, small and pointed, standing further apart, and comparatively unimportant. (Fig. 3.) In herbivorous animals, as the cow, the horse, &c., they are broad as in man, but varying in form and number. The canine or eye teeth human, (*c*, Fig. 2), are supposed by some anatomists to indicate that man is partly carnivorous ; but the same evidence would prove that the camel is still more carnivorous than man, because these teeth are proportionately

Fig. 3.

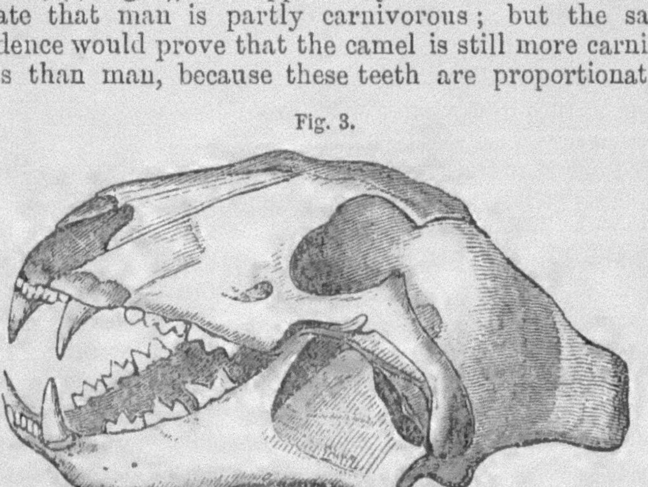

The skull of the Panther.

longer in that animal than in man. (Fig. 4.) The bicuspids, (b, Fig. 2), in man, have two prominences, but in

Fig. 4.

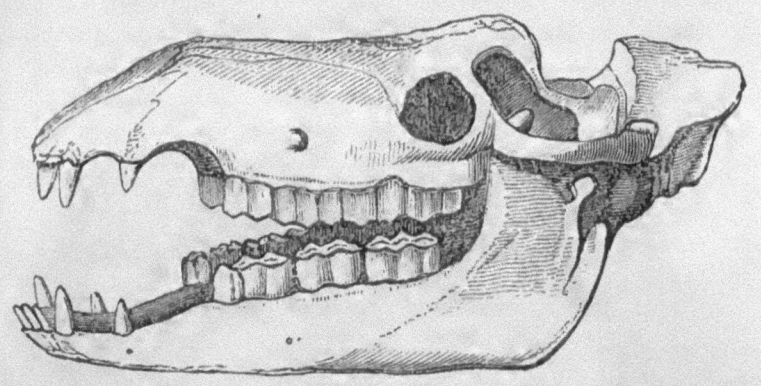

The skull of the Camel.

carnivorous animals they rise into sharp points like saw
teeth, (Fig. 3), much larger and more prominent than
those of man ; they present nothing of the grinding and
triturating surface which those of man and herbivorous
animals present ; but like their eye teeth, they are fit for
tearing and cutting. (Fig. 3.) The cheek teeth in the
lower jaw of man, like those of the herbivorous and frugivorous animals, are simply raised into rounded eleva-
tions, and are directly opposite to those of the upper jaw,

Fig. 5.

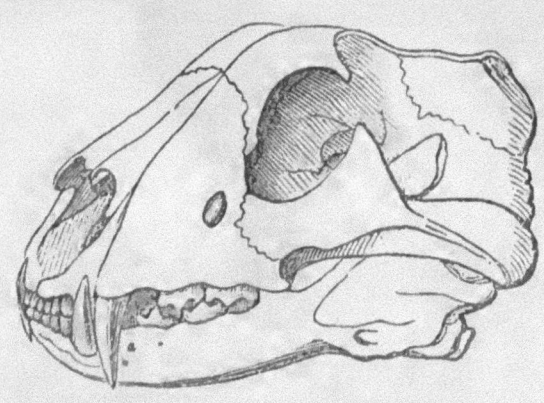

The Skull of the Tiger.

so as to mash and grind the substances that come between them ; but in carnivorous animals they shut between those of the upper jaw, so as to tear and cut the flesh on which they feed. When both series are viewed together, the general outline may be compared to a saw, and their action to that of a pair of shears. (Fig. 5.) The lateral motion

Fig. 6.

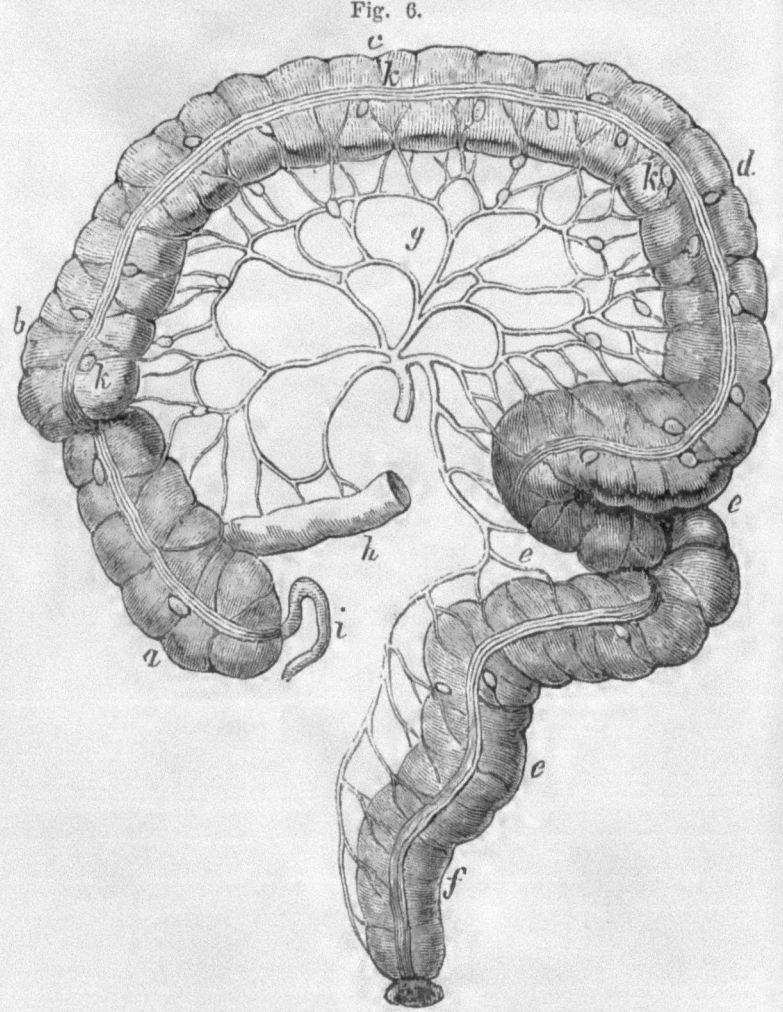

The Colon.

a, b, c, d, e. The colon.   f. Rectum.
e. sigmoid flexture.   h. Small intestine.
g. Vessels crossing the ucrocolon.

of the lower jaw of man, as in herbivorous animals, shows an adaptability to the grinding process which is necessary for grain, pulse, and vegetables, but which the jaws and structure of the teeth of carnivorous or omnivorous animals will not admit of. (Fig. 5.) The other alimentary organs, the stomach and alimentary canal, are in perfect accordance with man's teeth, adapted to a vegetable and farinaceous diet. The colon, (Fig. 6), like that of herbivorous animals, is large and deeply cellulated, whilst that of carnivorous animals is uniformly smooth. The external appearance, the limbs, mouth, nose, ears, eyes, head, face, hands, fingers, and nails; in fact, the whole structure of man, present no approximation to the appearance of a flesh-eating animal, uniting with all the senses in declaring the human constitution to be best adapted to subsist on the different productions of the soil.

Having given some insight into the nature of teeth, let us now proceed to the comparison of the digestive organs. The general rule of nature in the organization of animals is to give a simple stomach, having only a single cavity to carnivorous animals, and a compound one (composed of two or more distinct cavities to herbivorous animals). This rule has some apparent exceptions, as in the instance of the horse. Further, it is observed that generally the in-

Fig. 7.

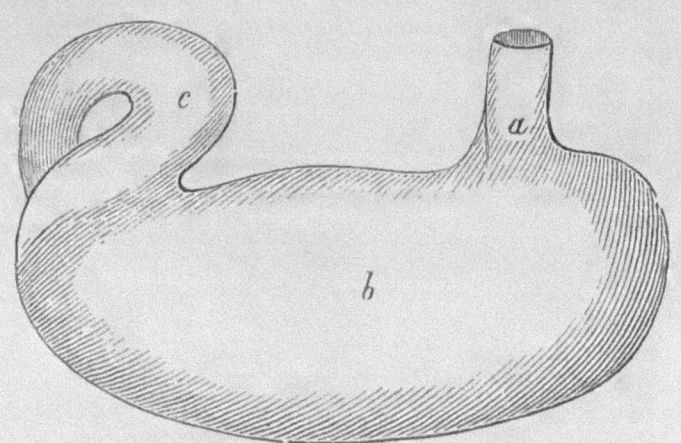

Stomach of the Lion.

a. The cardiac, or opening of the stomach, from the gullet.
b. The stomach.
c. The pylorus, or opening of the stomach into the intestine.

testines of carnivorous, and even omnivorous, animals are short, and those of herbivorous long. Illustrating these laws by animals in each class, it may be remarked that the stomach of the lion (Fig. 6) is of a simple construction, and that the intestines are about three times the length of the body.

The stomach of the sheep, as of other ruminating ani-

Fig. 8.

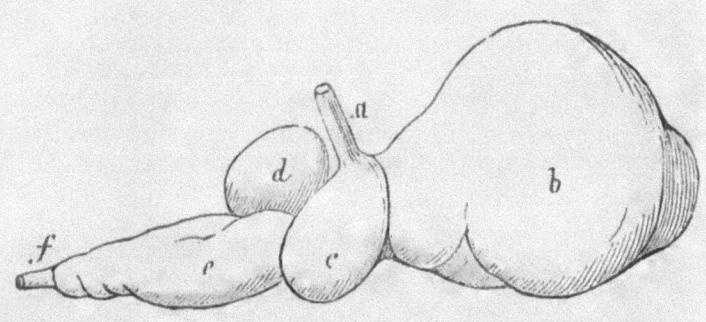

Stomach of Sheep.

a. The œsophagus.	*d*. Manyplies.
b. Paunch.	*e*. Abomasum, or true digestive cavity.
c. Honcycomb.	*f*. Pylorus.

mals (Fig. 8), consists of four portions, and the length of the intestinal canal is twenty-six times that of the body.

The stomach of man (Fig. 9) is also usually said to be simple, or single in its construction, which is an argument to exclude him from the class purely herbivorous; but as the process of digestion is not completed until the chyme has passed the duodenum, the latter might be considered a second stomach, and man would with equal reason be denied the use of flesh. And further, as the intestines are six times the length of the body, and measure, in the manner other animals are measured (that is exclusive of the limbs), twelve times the length of the body, he is certainly excluded even from the omnivorous order.

In the instance of the ourang-outang, the stomach is simple, and the relative length of the alimentary canal is somewhat shorter than in the human subject; but so close is the resemblance between the alimentary organs of that animal and of man, that a good anatomist might mistake the stomach and the small gut and colon of a large monkey for those of a man. In strict accordance with the established principles in the science of comparative anatomy, the alimentary organs of the ourang-outang are to be regarded as the true type with which we are to compare those of the human being, in order to ascertain

Fig. 9.

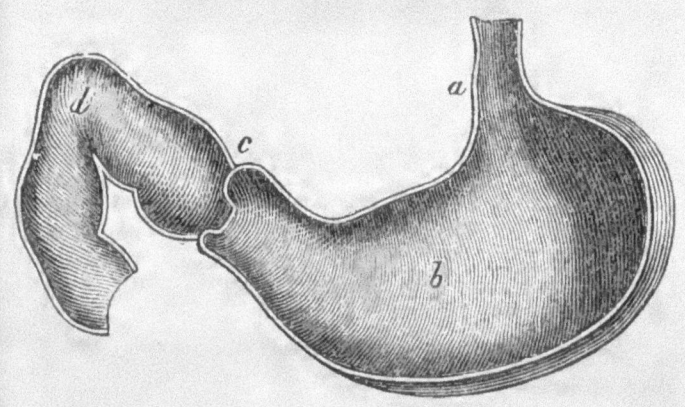

The Human Stomach.

a. Œsophagus.   c. Pyloric valve.
b. The stomach.   d. The duodenum.

the natural dietetic character of man. If, as is the fact, the ourang-outang, with teeth more canine than man's, subsists almost wholly on the products of the vegetable kingdom, there is less propriety in our custom of resorting to flesh as food.

Another fact of considerable importance in comparing the two classes is, that all purely herbivorous animals and the monkey tribes have porous skins, with an immense number of perspiratory glands, by which the superfluous heat, generated by an excess of non-azotized food escapes, the retention of which in the system would be injurious, which is also the case with man ; while, on the other hand, neither the carnivorous or omnivorous animals have porous skins, but the lungs are the only means of throwing off their impurities ; and it is not improbable that hydrophobia owes its origin to the inactivity of this function of the skin. The horse sweats through his skin ; the dog and pig never : therefore man has no relation to flesh-eaters. Some persons, having discovered apertures in the skins of carnivorous animals, have supposed them to be pores ; but they have mistaken the apertures of the hair for those of the pores (Fig. 10.)

Fig. 10.

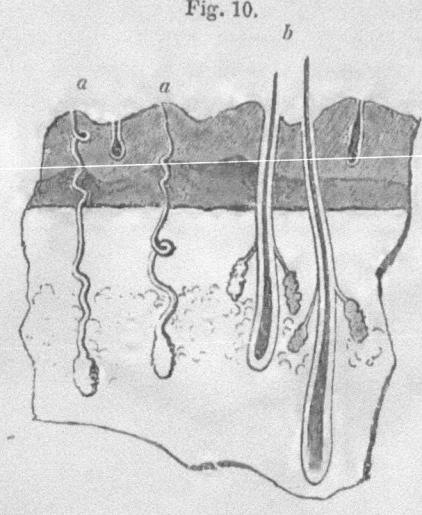

Microscopic View of the Hair Pores and Skin.
The dark ground represents the skin. *a*, the pores; and *b*, the hairs.

Let the reader take into consideration the facts, that in man there is the absence of the claws, and other offensive weapons ; the form of the incisor, cuspid, and molar teeth ; the articulation of the lower jaw ; the form of the zygomatic arch ; the size of the temporal and masseter muscles and salivary glands ; the length of the alimentary canal ; the size and internal structure of the colon and cœcum ; the size of the liver, and the perspiratory glands ; and he will see that in all these respects man closely resembles the herbivorous class of animals : while all the organs connected with alimentation are evidently very different from those of carnivorous animals ; his proper food being the corn and fruits of the earth.

We might greatly extend our comparisons, did not our space forbid ; but the arguments brought against this view of the subject, have been so often, and we think so successfully met, that with those who are at all familiar with the matter, they have become like old suits of masking attire in a Jew's shop ; so often used by the dirty and diseased, that a prudent man would hesitate to touch them ; and it would not be too much to say that it would be difficult to find a man of *principle*, well acquainted with comparative anatomy, in the present advanced stages of the science, who would resort to man's *organization* in support of the opinion that he is by *nature* a flesh-eater.

CHAPTER III.

ANALYTICAL CHEMISTRY.

THE question of feeding and fattening animals in the most economical way has largely engaged the attention and experiments of chemists of late years; and although not originally made with a view to building up the human structure, all the light which has been thrown on the subject by Liebig, Playfair, Boussingault, &c., has gone in favor of an exclusively vegetarian diet, as shown in the following table, which is deduced from the *facts* promulgated by the above authorities :—

TABLE OF THE AMOUNT OF NUTRIMENT AND COMPARATIVE COST OF VARIOUS ARTICLES OF DIET.

It will be obvious that, as the prices of food vary, the cost of a certain amount of nutriment from each will vary in like proportion. The prices given are taken from returns when food was plentiful and cheap, the flesh-meat being calculated as the lean of flesh, without either bone, fat, or membrane.

Read :—100 pounds of wheat contain 85 pounds of solid matter, and 14½ of water; and supply to the body 62 lbs. of heat-producing principles, with 2½ lbs. of earthy matter for the bones. The cost of 100 lbs being 9s 5¼d. The cost of 100 lbs. of nutriment from wheat being 11s. 0¼d., or of the flesh-forming principle alone—£2 4s. 11¼d. See " Products of the Vegetable Kingdom."

Articles of Diet.	Contain		Supply to Body			Comparative Cost			Mean Time occupied in Chymification according to Beaumont's Table.
	Solid Matter.	Water.	Carbonaceous or heat-producing principles.	Protenized or flesh-forming principles.	Earthy matter for the bones.	Price per 100 lbs.	Cost of Nutriment per 100 lbs.	Cost of Flesh-forming principle per 100 lbs.	
						£ s. d.	£ s. d.	£ s. d.	
Wheat ..	85	14½	62	21	2½	0 9 5¼	0 11 0¼	2 4 11¼	3h. 15m.
Oats	82	18	68	11	3	0 7 6½	0 9 2½	3 8 6½	3 30
Peas	84	16	51½	29	3½	0 10 5	0 12 4¾	1 15 11	
Beans	86	14	51½	31	3½	0 6 11¾	0 8 1¼	1 2 6	2 30 boiled
Barley-ml.	84½	15½	68½	14	2	0 6 3	0 7 4¾	2 4 7½	{ 2 0 boiled { 1 30 soup
Maize-ml .	90	10	77	11	2	0 7 3	0 7 6	3 3 0	
Rice	92	8	82	8	2	1 4 6	1 7 0	15 0 0	1 0 boiled
Sago	88	12	84	3·4	..	1 9 0	1 12 6	41 3 8	1 45 boiled
Potatoes .	28	72	25	2	1	0 1 5¾	0 5 3¼	3 13 11½	2 30 { boiled or roasted
Carrots ..	13	87	10	2	1	0 2 0¼	0 15 6½	5 1 0½	3 15 boiled
Turnips ..	11	89	9	1	1	0 0 8½	0 6 5¼	3 10 10	3 30 boiled
Beet Root	11	89	8½	1½	1	0 1 3	0 10 9	3 18 0	3 45 boiled
Veal	25	75	..	25	..	2 14 2	10 16 8	10 16 8	4 30 fried
Beef	25	75	..	25	..	2 18 4	11 13 4	11 13 4	from 3 to 4 30
Mutton ..	25	75	..	25	..	2 18 4	11 13 4	11 13 4	3 0 { boiled or broiled
Lamb	25	75	..	25	..	3 15 0	15 0 0	15 0 0	2 30 broiled

Nothing is more common than for medical books and writers to tell us that animal food is more *nutritious*, more *concentrated*, and more *digestible* than vegetarian. But these terms are generally employed without any very precise meaning. The truth is, in many cases, quite the contrary. If we determine the relative value of foods strictly by the rule of chemical analysis, according to the Liebig school, we shall find that good wheaten bread, rice, beans, peas, and lentils, contain four times as much nutritive virtue as the best flesh meat, while even the potato contains at least an equal amount. If we admit Liebig's theory of the combustion of carbon to sustain the animal temperature, we shall find abundance of carbon, and the *best kind* of carbon, in vegetarian food. And if we subscribe to the doctrine of the *nitrogenous* and *non-nitrogenous* distinctions of alimentary principles, we find nitrogen supplied in nearly all kinds of vegetation, and an inexhaustible supply, in case of accidental scarcity in the vegetable kingdom, in the atmosphere which surrounds us.

The table given above shows that flesh meat is not so nutritive as various vegetable products. The best flesh containing only 25 per cent. of solid matter, various vegetable productions containing from 70 to 90 per cent. Besides, it was found that whilst flesh supplied principally but one kind of nutriment, where three kinds were required, vegetable productions contained from 50 to 80 per cent. of another ingredient, which flesh, except as to its portion of fat, did not contain at all, besides extra ashes for the bones. Then it was said that the nutriment of flesh was superior; but the researches of Liebig have incontestably established that all the elements of nutrition originate in the vegetable kingdom; so that in partaking of flesh, men have to take the very vegetable principles, through the bodies of animals, which they could have directly from the bosom of nature. "Grain, and other nutritious vegetables yield us," said Liebig, "not only in starch, sugar, and gum, the carbon which protects our organs from the action of oxygen, and produces in the organism the heat which is essential to life, but also in the form of vegetable fibrine, albumen and caseine, our blood, from which the other parts of our body are developed." "These important products of vegetation are especially abundant in the seeds of the different kinds of grain, and of peas, beans, and lentils, and in the roots and juices of what are commonly called vegetables. They exist,

however, in all plants, without exception, and in every
part of plants, in larger or smaller quantity." Again :—
" Vegetable fibrine and animal fibrine, vegetable albumen
and animal albumen, hardly differ, even in form ; if these
principles be wanting in the food, the nutrition of the
animal is arrested ; and when they are present, the gra-
minivorous animal obtains in its food the very same principles on the presence of which the nutrition of the
carnivora entirely depends."

Dr. LYON PLAYFAIR, while admitting there may be difference in external appearance and in structure, asserts
that in their "ultimate structure there is none," and to
" render this more obvious," he subjoins the " composition
of these various substances, as obtained by different chemists, who executed their analysis without any knowledge
of the results obtained by the others :"—

	Gluten from Flour. BOUSSINGAULT	Cascin from Peas. SCHERER.	Albumen from Eggs. JONES.	Ox Blood. PLAYFAIR.	Ox Flesh. PLAYFAIR.
Carbon ...	54.2	54.138	55.000	54.35	54.12
Hydrogen	7.5	7.156	7.073	7.50	7.89
Nitrogen	13.9	15.672	15.920	15.76	15.67
Oxygen ...	24.4	23.034	22.007	22 39	22.32
	100.0	100.00	100.00	100.00	100.00

So that the good old book, rightly understood, after all,
confirms the truths of science ; for long since *it* asserted,
" All flesh is grass."

It is found that all parts of the food which can form
blood, and thus renew the animal structure of the body,
are due to the protein compounds, which have their sole
origin in the vegetable kingdom ; and thus the nutritive
parts of vegetables and flesh being identical, the popular
opinion of the peculiar characteristics of the nutriment of
the flesh of animals is altogether erroneous, the nutritive
particles of flesh being due to the ultimate elements of
nutrition derived from the vegetable food on which the
animals consumed have fed, as shewn by Liebig.

" Vegetables produce in their organism the blood of all
animals, for the carnivora in consuming the blood and
flesh of the graminivora, consume, strictly speaking, only

the vegetable principles which have served for the nutrition of the latter."

Why do we not act as rationally in body-building as we do in house-building? The former is more important. When we build a house we seek for a good foundation, employ the best workmen, and procure new materials. But in building up the body, which should be "the temple of the Holy Ghost," and presented "a *living* sacrifice, *holy* and acceptable to God, which is our reasonable service," flesh-eaters take the half worn out materials—the flesh of once living animals—and thus in an imperfect way the young of both sexes build up, and those arrived at maturity, repair the daily waste of their systems. No wonder, therefore, that the house is so small, so ill formed, so badly answers its purposes, and so soon falls into decay. To suppose the Creator had so constructed the masticatory, digestive, or the assimilating apparatus of man as to render him dependent upon the machinery of another animal for the preparation of his food, would be very humiliating to man, if it did not reflect on the wisdom or power of his Maker. It does not appear likely that so important an article as food, which supplies this mind-machine, can be taken in any form more perfect than that in which nature has provided it. Our best chemists have shown that while much remains in mystery as to what life is, and how it is maintained, the elements of its nourishment are readily obtained from the products of the vegetable kingdom, consisting of the nitrogenized and non-nitrogenized; the former being capable of being converted into muscle and organic matter, the latter being transformed into the elements of respiration.

The following are amongst the elements of nutrition :— Vegetable fibrine, albumen, and caseine, animal flesh and blood for carnivora. Elements of respiration — Starch, gum, cane sugar, grape sugar, sugar of milk for the young, a diseased product.

As muscle is formed only by the gluten or albumen of the food, which albumen is in reality flesh itself, we can ascertain the comparative value of food producing muscle :

100 lbs. of	Albumen.	Unazotd. matter.	100 lbs. of	Albumen.	Unazotd. matter.
Flesh	25	0	Oats	11	68
Blood	20	0	Barley-meal	14	68½
Beans	31	51½	Turnips	1	9
Peas	29	51½	Carrots	2	10
Lentils	33	48	Red-beet	1½	8½
Potatoes	2	25			

Dr. Lyon Playfair.

CHAPTER IV.

HUMAN PHYSIOLOGY.

THIS is the doctrine of the functions, showing us how the organism works and is acted upon by the food and various surrounding influences. It explains the actions and uses of the various tissues, nerves, 'and muscles ; how they are manufactured and preserved in health ; reveals to us a thousand wonders connected with our yet unfathomed nature ; and points out the laws and conditions we must obey if we would secure length of days, and a healthful and happy existence. Physiology, therefore, teaches us that food is the basis of the chyme, chyle, and blood ; and that blood is the basis of the entire organism : that the best food (other circumstances being equal) makes the best chyme, chyle, and blood ; and the best blood the best body and mind. Every organ of the human body is admirably adapted to the collection, preparation, and distribution of proper food, so that the whole man may be well developed : and *that* must be the *best food* for any species of animal which can build up the *best structure* without unduly taxing the energy of any one organ. Let us see how animal food acts on the stomach. It unduly taxes it, in consequence of its requiring a larger expenditure of energy to dispose of, or render it fit to pass from the stomach : thus it is that, in addition to the exciting nature of such food, a considerable degree of constitutional disturbance is set up during the process of its digestion, and the whole system is subject to a species of *miniature fever* at each meal. But can any one imagine that the great and good Author of our being has designed that we should be thrown into a fever (a disease) once, or twice, or three times every day of our lives ? We need not wonder that the majority of our countrymen suffer from indigestion, and its numerous attendants. The wonder would be were it otherwise. Not only is the stomach injured, but the healthy character of the chyle is interfered with. BEAUMONT, OLIVER, MAJENDIE, and others assert that chyme formed from the products of the vegetable kingdom can be preserved from putrefaction nine days longer than that formed from a mixed diet. This may be accounted for from the fact of its greater purity, and hence greater vitality, and as a consequence the blood is also of a superior character, and less liable to be affected by the noxious influences by which man is surrounded. The influence of a vegetarian diet is also remarkable on *the heart*, arising from the same cause. The principal function of the heart is to regulate and sustain the circulation of the blood, but its pulsations are governed, to a considerable extent, by the state of the general organism, and especially of the blood. If feverish excitement be present, either in the blood, or any of the organs, and they become diseased, the sympathetic nerves carry intelligence to the brain, and it becomes excited, and the action of the heart increased, and as a consequence an increased amount of blood is sent through the arteries and veins, nature thus seeking to prevent or repair the mischief. Nothing is, perhaps, better proved than that the duration of human life, as a general rule, is in proportion to the activity of the pulse ; and that persons who reach an advanced life have had a pulse comparatively slow. There are some exceptions to this rule, into which we cannot enter—but the rule holds good. Having paid some attention to this matter, the result is, that I have always found the pulse of an established vegetarian, whose other habits were good, ranging from 50 to 60, while that of others would be from 70 to 90, or more. Provided the pulse is firm and regular, it cannot be too slow for the purposes of health and longevity. But we glance at the effects of flesh-eating on the lungs, the great organs in which the air purifies and vitalizes the blood. The oftener, and the more impure the blood is sent into the lungs, the more oxygen they will require, and therefore the oftener we must inspire and respire ; and as a consequence, the harder the lungs must work. As the blood is sent from the heart it is believed to pass through not less than 174 millions of arteries, by which it is distributed to every part of the body, whence it is drawn back again to the heart through another 174 millions of vessels, or tubes, called veins, taking up in its passage as much as possible of the worn out, morbid matters of the system, which it takes to the lungs, where it is poured into 174 millions of air cells, in which the air purifies and vitalizes it. Here again we discover one, and, perhaps, a principal cause of the numerous cases of consumption with which our people are afflicted. On the other hand, if vegetarianism gives these two important organs seasons of comparative rest, and never overworks them, it is only natural to infer they will do their work better, and retain their capabilities longer ; or, in other words, we shall be healthier and live longer. As a result of being healthier, we shall be larger and stronger. And how do facts bear us out here ? Remarkably well. Before vegetarianism was much talked about, and not with a view to establish it, Professor Forbes, and others, at Edinburgh, measured, weighed, and tested the strength of a given number of Englishmen, Scotchmen, and Irishmen, they being pretty much in the same walks of life. They were taken at about the age of 25. The results were—

ENGLISH			SCOTCH.			IRISH.		
Height inches	Weight. lbs.	Strngth lbs.	Hgh. in	Wgh. lbs.	Strngth lbs.	Hgh. In.	Wgh. lbs.	Strngh. lbs.
68.9	151	403	69	152	423	70	155	432

Thus showing, in each case, the inferiority of the beefeating English, and the superiority of the potato-fed Irish.

All the secretions of the vegetarians are more pure, bland, and copious, and the excretions—the sweat, urine, fecal matter, &c.—are less offensive to the senses : their teeth are less affected with tartarous incrustations, and their breath is mostly if not entirely free from the rank odour so common to flesh-eaters. The vegetarian can always endure hunger and thirst longer, without loss of strength, and sustain privation of food with less suffering than flesh-eaters. His appetite is invariably good, while a flesh-eater's often fails. Digestion with the former is quiet, unattended with irritation, oppression, and dulness. All the mental passions of the vegetarians are more governable : the firmest and most vigorous structures of body are found amongst them : they possess more elasticity of body and mind ; and when fatigued by excessive toil, they recover sooner and more completely. Extremes of heat and cold are better endured : they seldom present the extreme of fat or leanness. All the senses, tasting, smelling, hearing, seeing, and feeling—are more healthfully acute, and less morbidly sensitive, than those of the flesh-eaters. Bodily symmetry and personal beauty have always distinguished those who have subsisted mainly on vegetable food from those whose principal diet has been animal food, *other circumstances being equal.* We beg to call special attention to the close of the last sentence, which must be taken into account in *all* our observations.

CHAPTER V.

NATIONAL HISTORIES.

THERE is no reason to believe that our first parents departed from their vegetarian habits; although the children of men went astray in an early period of their history, "by dipping their tongues in gore," and a large proportion of the human family has continued in the transgression ever since. But there havebeen, at all times, men of superior intelligence and high-toned morality, who have rigidly abstained from strong drinks and from flesh-eating, as well as from the other health-destroying habits which are often engendered by indulgence in flesh and alcohol. Among these abstainers, it is remarkable, that we always find the ancient poets, philosophers, and prophets, who were distinguished alike for "temperance in all things," purity of life, rectitude of deportment, and length of years. At the earliest and most happy period of human existence of which we have any record, the vegetarian practice was a rule of life; and all nations, in proportion as they have approached it, other conditions being equal, have exhibited superior health, strength, and longevity. Of the truth of these statements, all history, sacred and profane, furnishes us with ample illustrations. In the sacred, we refer particularly to the *appointment* in GENESIS, the *facts* in EXODUS and DANIEL, and the *Prophecy* in ISAIAH; and generally to the whole history of the Jews, which show that for the first 2000 years of their history, excepting at their feasts and on great occasions, they were vegetarians, in accordance with their 40 years' training in the wilderness. The ancient Egyptians, also, among whom the Jews had so long sojourned, and who were amongst the most enlightened and most enduring nations of the age, were in the main vegetarians : so were the ancient Persians, Romans, and Greeks, in the days of their greatest glory.

Pythagoras raised up a society of vegetarians 550 years before Christ. He was a very learned man, and a great philosopher, whose chief object was to exalt the intellectual and moral condition of his disciples, who are said to have been exceedingly numerous, in almost all quarters of the then known world, especially in Greece and Italy. A school of 600 was established at Crotona, in South Italy, besides numerous other schools in various parts. They were much persecuted, as reformers ever have been :

Pythagoras died not of disease, but of starvation, at 80, in a place where he had sought a retreat from the fury of his enemies. Josephus testified that the Essenes, a sect of the ancient Jews, numbering several thousands, were healthy and long-lived because of their regular mode of life and simplicity of diet, which Pliny tells us consisted of the fruit of the palm tree. It is certain, however, they were vegetarians after the Pythagorean philosophy. The Brahmin priests, who are a very numerous sect, are all very strict vegetarians.

But it is a fact, which no intelligent historian will dispute, that the healthiest, best tempered, and longest-lived ; the most robust and enduring labourers, of all ages and countries, whether men or animals, have ever been, and still are, in the main vegetarians. Take animals, and compare the temper, health, long life, and the capability of enduring prolonged toil, in the flesh-eaters and the vegetarians, and we fear not for the result. The same will apply to human beings. The peasantry of England, Scotland, Ireland, Italy, Turkey, Greece, Germany, Switzerland, France, Spain, Portugal, Norway, Sweden, Denmark, Poland, and many parts of Russia, subsist principally, and many of them entirely, on vegetarian food ; and the finest specimens of health, strength, and activity, are found among those portions of the peasantry of several of the above countries, who use no flesh meat at all. Almost the entire of the Japanese of the interior live on rice and fruit, and the concurrent testimony of all geographers and travellers is, that in their physical and intellectual development at least, to say nothing of their moral peculiarities, they are the finest men in all Asia; indeed they are scarcely behind the middle nations of Europe. Nearly the same remarks will apply to China, and, with little modification, to Hindostan, whose inhabitants use so little animal food that it may be regarded as a seasoning rather than a substantial part of their diet. The Georgians and the Circassians, the natives of Otaheite, Sandwich, and Pitcairn's Islands, the people of the Marquesas and Washington Islands, the Indians of Mexico, on the Tobasco, the Polish and Hungarian peasants from the Carpathian Mountains, the Spaniards of Rio Salado, in South America, and the Peruvians, the slaves of Brazil, the labourers of Laguoiro, the Moorish porters of Gibraltar, and the porters of Terceira and Smyrna, subsist mostly on coarse, plain, vegetable food, and they are among the most beautiful as well as the most hardy and enduring people on earth many of them possess a most powerful muscular development, and can carry singly from 200 to 800 lbs. weight.

Compare these with the Laplanders, Ostiacs, Samoides, Tungooses, Burats, Kamtschatdales, and Esquimaux, in the north of Europe, Asia, and America; the natives of Siberia and Terra del Fuego; the people of Anderman's Island; the natives of New Holland and Van Dieman's Land, and the Calmuc Tartars, who all possess a low, deformed, and semi-brutal organization; some of them being stunted and dwarfish, others coarse, rough, and hideous. Their principal food is fish, flesh, and every kind of animal fats and oils which they are able to procure. It should be remarked, too, that the intellectual and moral constitution of these inferior races of men is as degraded and depraved as is their bodily organization. Excepting these few, meagre, weak, timid nations, and the wealthier and middle classes of every country where flesh is eaten, who are able to range lawlessly over the Creator's domains, and select for their tables whatever fancy or fashion, or a capricious appetite may dictate, or physical power afford them, the masses of the people, especially in agricultural districts, are mainly vegetarians. In short, considerably more than one-half are vegetarians, either from necessity or choice; and many of the others take so little as to have hardly any effect on their structure or character. And it is remarkable, as we noticed in the case of the ancient Persians, Egyptians, Romans, and Greeks, that as *they* departed from a pure mode of living, so their physical, mental, moral, and national greatness departed; so in more modern times with nations and with families. The luxuriant die out; and were it not that their places and positions are replenished by the more temperate of the middle classes, and these again by the still more temperate of the so-called lower classes, national bankruptcy, in regard to physical, mental, and moral wealth would inevitably ensue. Come, however, it must, sooner or later, without reform. A flesh-eating, alcohol, tea and coffee drinking, and tobacco-smoking nation, may retain the supremacy of the world for a short time, as several European and American nations have done; just as the man or the horse, whose brain and nerves are stimulated by strong drink, flesh, or the whip and spur, may for a time retain —through the medium of an artificial strength—the ascendancy over their competitors; but "the triumph of the wicked [those who break the law] is short;" and their subsequent [punishment] debility will be proportionate.

CHAPTER VI.

INDIVIDUAL EXPERIENCE.

Dr. Alcott, in his "Vegetable Diet, as sanctioned by Medical Men in all Ages," has given a remarkable list of individual cases, such as would astonish the generality of Englishmen, who, because they have read little, and travelled less, are apt to suppose that everybody is as much enslaved to beer and beef as they are. We are apt to believe very little beyond our own experience, and those of us who take credit for a tolerable share of faith in theories and principles, will generally find that experience has had more or less to do with the convictions we have formed ; and that when a system is presented with which we have had no experimental acquaintance, we are apt to curl the lip, and regard it as beneath our attention. This is unphilosophical.

Reader ! you have your own little world of thought, action, and experience. Do not mistake its evidence on any, especially on this subject, for the credence of that larger world which comprehends the thought, action, and experience of more capacious intellects than your own. We ask you to examine the facts and evidence in favor of a Vegetarian diet, and then honestly and fairly to put the system to a practical test. You will then have the benefit of an experience in the matter. We admit individual experience could have little influence in deciding any question in the mind of a second person ; but when the experiment has been made, *successfully, by such a large number of such persons* as will be found in the following list, it is, we think, sufficient to induce an experiment in your own case ; for, after all, this is an individual experimental matter, and no person is, or can be, in a proper position to decide the relative merits of the questions at issue, unless he has tested the matter for himself. It is nature's own method. Theory can never teach a child to walk ; it must "feel its own weight" on its own feet ; and the apprentice must *work* at the trade he wishes to be master of.

The time when experiments in diet can best be made is in early life, before the constitution has become tainted by a corrupt mode of living. But in all experiments which are made, care should be taken as to the manner in which it is done, and due regard should be paid to the relative proportions of corn, fruits, and vegetables used. The change should also be made gradually, if flesh has been used freely. If you have taken it rather freely twice or thrice a day, begin your trials by taking a smaller quantity at each meal for a week ; then leave it off at one of the meals altogether, and thus the system will become accustomed to the change without any disagreeable feelings or consequences.

In addition to the cases cited under the head of " National Histories," the experience of Daniel and his companions, Pythagoras and his disciples, Numa, Socrates, Plato, Epictetus, Epicurus, Porphery, Plutarch, John the Baptist, and many others of the devotees of philosophy and humanity of ancient times, were zealous advocates of vegetarianism, under various names ; while the modern list of disciples to this form of truth is scarcely less illustrious—persons with whom no one has cause to be ashamed to be found in company—for it contains the names of Milton, Tryon, Swedenborg, Wesley, Franklin, Cheyne, Howard, John Nicholson, Shelley, T. Newton, Sir Isaac Newton, Lamb, Jackson, Sir Richard Phillips, Lamartine, Greaves, the Abbe Gullani, Peter Gassendi, Shillitoe, Mussey, Jennings, Sewall, Whitlaw, Cowherd, Graham, Allcott, Shew, Trall, Metcalf, Fowler, Smith, and Simpson ; besides many other living illustrious men in America, and in our own country. These men have all been, or are, promoters of the world's progress, and will be remembered with respect and gratitude by the millions who benefit by their labours. Their lives present examples of the beneficial influence of the experiments they made in relation to diet.

But we shall be told that these experiments have been made chiefly by persons who "lived long ago," and we are asked for present cases. These we have spread all over the flesh-eating countries of England and America—living evidences that health and vigour are promoted and sustained beyond the common lot of men ; for besides thousands who are practising the system of Vegetarianism without belonging to the Society, there is enrolled in its ranks a respectable number of persons, in the various walks of life, whose experience and practice prove the decided advantage of the reformed system of dietetics. See more on this subject under the head of *the Rise and Progress of the Vegetarian Society.*

CHAPTER VII.

REMEDIAL TENDENCIES.

DR. THACKRAH, one of our best medical writers, asserts that "Errors in diet are the great source of disease; amendment of diet is the basis of recovery;" and he is borne out by facts. Health depends, first, upon a sound constitution, built up of good materials; and secondly, upon a proper employment of that organization; therefore, disease is generally the consequence of a defect in one or both of these. Health and disease are not contingencies, but are governed by laws, as immutable as those which rule the planets. Nor is disease natural to man, or the arbitrary infliction of Providence; but it is the result of the violation of organic laws. Those laws are capable of being known, understood, and obeyed by every human being, and consequently, more or less of health may be enjoyed by all. It is a great absurdity to suppose that healthy persons are as much exposed to attacks of disease as others. A healthy person is *physically* in the same position as JESUS CHRIST was *morally*, when He said "Satan cometh and findeth nothing [no moral taint] in me." So the healthy man; disease cometh and findeth no affinity—no *nidus* for its reception. HOWARD, it is known, was a vegetarian for the last forty years of his life, yet went through every form of exposure to disease, contagious and otherwise, perfectly unharmed. GEN. T. SHELDON, of the United States, spent several years in the most sickly parts of the southern States, with an entire immunity from disease; and thought it did not matter where persons were if their dietetic and other habits were correct. And S. GRAHAM remarks that "Under a proper regimen men may go to New Orleans or Liberia, or anywhere else they choose, and yet enjoy good health." And facts favour this opinion; for during the prevalence of cholera, both in England and America, from its first visit in 1832 till the last, either wholly escaped, or were very slightly attacked by the complaint, and yet some of them were very much exposed to it.

The erroneous notion that healthy persons are more exposed than others, arises from another and very common error, viz.: those who are regarded by the superficial and short-sighted in this matter, as the most robust and healthy, are usually those whose unhealthy habits have sown the seeds of disease ; and nothing is wanting but the usual circumstances of epidemics to rouse them into action. The train is laid, and only requires the touch-paper to produce an explosion. Facts prove that these so-called strong, healthy persons, with full color, and gorged blood-vessels, are almost sure to die whenever disease attacks them. It is now an admitted fact, that our domesti-cated fatted animals are generally diseased ; that their diseased condition is not readily detected ; and that persons feeding on such flesh must partake of the disease of the animal on which they feed. And although fruits, corn, and vegetables may be diseased, that diseased condition is readily detected, and hence the article is rejected. Here is one great danger to the flesh-eater, and security to the vegetarian. The history of all those persons and nations, both of ancient and modern date, confirms us in these views —all showing that as man returns to nature, in his diet, and habits, disease is removed, his health becomes im-proved, and confirmed, even to a good old age.

Look at the question in a curative point of view. The case of L. Carnaro is familiar to most. In the 2nd vol. of the *Medical Transactions*, article 18, is the case of Thomas Wood, a miller, of Billericay, Essex. In the year 1764, when he was 45 years of age, he was overwhelmed with a complication of terrible disorders. On reading the life of Carnaro, he left off intoxicating drinks, and finally animal food, taking, at last, only one pound of flour boiled, and one pint and a half of skimmed milk per day. He took considerable exercise, and, to use his own words, having thus disposed of the incumbrance of ten or eleven stone weight of distempered flesh and fat, he became metamor-phosed from a monster to a person of moderate size— from the condition of an unhealthy, decrepit old man, to perfect health, and to the vigor and activity of youth, and could carry a quarter of a ton weight, which he could not do at the age of 30. His usual pulse beat only from 44 to 47 per minute : he had little or no sensible perspiration, even when taking severe and long continued exercise. Another case is reported by Mr. Rowbottom, surgeon, of Stockport, in the *Lancet*, of 1842, as follows :—" The son of a Mr. Fielding, of that town, about three years old, had been ill eighteen months. He was covered from head to foot with ulcers ; his eyes, nose, ears, mouth, and, in fact, his whole head and face were involved in one complete mass of fetid running sores and ulcers, so that his little thighs seemed nearly separating from his body. For more than twelve months he had been quite blind, and had never been able to sit down, even on a pillow, but stood upon his feet, and leaned upon his elbow upon the nurse. He had scarcely been able to lie in bed for the whole time. Eight of the most eminent medical men had given him up as incurable, and some of them declared that no known mortal power could even improve his condition, much less effect a cure. From certain views which I held on the origin of disease, I was induced to recommend a diet consisting almost entirely of ripe fruits and honey, or sugar and treacle. The child commenced this diet on the 13th of September, 1841. He had stewed fruits, &c., to all his meals, and was allowed frequently to eat grapes, cherries, plums, apples, pears, and such other fruit as could be obtained. On the 16th (only three days) the sores on his back were beginning to disappear : on the 23rd he was very sensibly improved ; and on the 1st of January, 1842, not a single ulcer remained on his body ; the skin became remarkably clean and fair, and the features, which for twelve months had been in such a state that it was impossible to do more than guess at the position of his nose and eyes, were restored to their wonted appearance."

These facts might be multiplied by thousands, from the history of the vegetarian negroes of the West Indies, China, and Hindostan, showing that they recover from all kinds of accidents more rapidly than any flesh-eating Europeans ; and should at least create strong suspicion that our diseases, if not caused, are much exasperated by our flesh-eating habits. The records of disease and premature decay in this country are truly appalling. The unnecessary waste of life in England and Wales may be fairly estimated at 40,000 annually, accompanied by not less than 750,000 cases of sickness. Think of 40,000 persons sacrificed annually, chiefly between the age of 20 and 40—of nearly 100,000 widows receiving out-door relief ; these have 150,000 fatherless children depending on them, besides 20,000 orphan children in our unions ; and notwithstanding that half the children born in this country die before they are eight years of age, and before they have, as we can conceive, answered any one purpose on the great theatre of life. Do we not reflect on the wisdom and goodness of God when we say these things accord with His will ? We believe flesh-eating is at the bottom of this fearful sacrifice of human life : as we see nothing of the sort amongst vegetarian nations or vegetarian families.

CHAPTER VIII.

POLITICAL ECONOMY.

THE *Liverpool Journal* made the following statement some time since :—"Those who tell us that we can feed all our people at home, talk nonsense. We cannot." This was asserted on the ground of *surplus population*, which we assert has no existence, inasmuch as we are quite capable of giving remunerative "employment to sixty-four millions of persons on the land alone, and abundance of the best food to 256 millions of inhabitants of the United Kingdom of Great Britain and Ireland," without importing a single grain of corn. The facts recorded in the last Chapter relative to disease, deaths, and pauperism in this country are truly appalling. How to meet these frightful evils, and to provide labour and food for the whole population, is a problem which must be solved. CARLYLE, in his "Past and Future," says, this is "the problem of the whole future." Wise legislation may do much to lessen the evils, and therefore we regret that many of our legislators, who when asked, "What means do you propose for the permanent remunerative employment of the people ?" are compelled, as was Mr. Denison, to say, We don't know. The Temperance Movement is effecting immense good. The Inclosure Scheme is rendering the soil more productive. Since the reign of George III. it has brought under cultivation nearly nine millions of acres of land, and with improved culture they have augmented the value of landed property to the extent of nearly nine millions sterling, as well as increased our average annual crop of corn from twenty millions to thirty millions of quarters : but the great *panacea* now recommended is *Emigration*. We differ *in toto* from the *Liverpool Journal.* If the people continue to fatten and eat cattle, we readily agree that we "cannot feed our people ;" but we demur to the *necessity* or *policy* of thus occupying the soil of our country.

We do not husband our resources. Adopt the Vegetarian System at once, and we shall not only vastly improve in health, strength, sobriety, intellectuality, and morality ; but we shall have "bread enough and to spare," even with ten times the amount of our present population. But this is not all ; vegetarianism augments the comforts of its votaries, by increasing their means of subsistence : while it produces thoughtfulness and providence in the management of their own affairs, and a feeling of humanity towards others. There will be less *selfishness*, extravagance, and competitiveness, which will prevent reckless marriages, and thus put *natural* checks upon the excessive increase of population.

A very large portion of land now in pasturage, and for the growth of hops and barley for malt, might grow food for man. Those who have never carefully examined the subject, have no conception of the number of people which a certain quantity of land, well cultivated, and its produce properly husbanded, will sustain on vegetarian principles. The difference when compared with that of mixed diet is astonishing. This is a very grave question. We learn that during the last forty years our population has increased at the rate of 15 per cent. in ten years ; and consequently doubled its numbers in about 66 years. Therefore, should wars, disease, and other checks, interfere no more than they have recently done with this well-ascertained law, the next 150 years, 100 millions will be the population of Great Britain and Ireland. How are these to be fed on any other plan than the vegetarian ? ALISON states that " On the most moderate calculation, Great Britain and Ireland are capable of maintaining 120 millions in ease and affluence."

The estimated produce of an acre of land is, of mutton, 228 lbs. per year, or 10 oz. per day ; beef, 182½ lbs. per year, or 8 ozs. per day ; wheat, 1526 lbs. per year, or 4 lbs. per day ; potatoes, 22,400 lbs. per year, or 61 lbs. per day. But Dr. Knight informs us, that a small plantation of early ash-leaved kidney potatoes, which are not the best bearers, produced 665 bushels of 80 lbs. each per acre, or 146 lbs. per day ; and by Mr. Rawson's improved mode of culture, 34,122 lbs. per acre, or 93 lbs. per day, of the red-nosed kidney have been obtained. Take then 64 millions of acres of land capable of *spade* husbandry ; appropriate 15 millions of acres to wheat, which will support more than 45 millions of people ; 15 millions more to potatoes, which will amply provide for ten persons per acre, or 150 millions ; thus you have a supply for 195 millions, and have yet more than one-half of the available land unoccupied, or occupied in producing all the fruits and delicacies of the climate.

Here there are resources almost illimitable ; and when science shall have shed its meridian light upon the production and husbanding of food, then trees, shrubs, and herbs will lend assistance in producing a still greater variety of wholesome and nutritious sustenance for man.

CHAPTER IX.

DOMESTIC ECONOMY.

POLITICAL Economy teaches us to view matters nationally, and generally; Domestic Economy relates more particularly to individuals and families. Having examined the remarks and facts of the preceding Chapter, let us see how they apply to the domestic circle. All schemes which have for their object the amelioration of the human family may be tested by their relative simplicity and their approximation to that standard of all natural operations— Economy. The whole system of the universe is based on a rigid recognition of economy. Every law pertaining either to matter or spirit has economy for its basis. All the modes of nature are simple; the revolutions of globes, the growth of worlds and of flowers, the development of physical perfection through long trains of metamorphoses, are all regulated and controlled by the great law of economy. There is no waste in nature; from the moss which grows on the stubborn rock, to the finest trees which grace our fertile soil, every plant, every tree, every leaf and fibre, has its appropriate service to perform in the wise and rigid economy of nature. Not only is this doctrine taught us by Providence, but it was exemplified by Jesus Christ, when he commanded his disciples to " gather up the fragments that nothing be lost."

So, every law pertaining to man's position on the earth; every condition tending to the consummation of his happiness, is governed by the same simplicity and economy. While he observes the institutions of his nature, his life is simple, tranquil, and serene; but if he abuse his moral liberty, by the adoption of habits at variance with his organization, his existence becomes interwoven and complex, the simplicity and economy, which live in every true act of his life, no longer pervade them; he falls into a condition in which he is a stranger to physical health and enjoyment, and is no longer a recipient of the elevating influences of moral and religious peace.

The purposes for which food is required in the body are, first, to supply materials for respiration, and secondly, to supply materials for the regeneration of the frame, or in other words, to infuse new particles into those tissues which have been worn down by the action of the muscular and nervous systems. To supply the first, we require daily about 12ozs. of carbon ; and for the second, about 350 grs. of nitrogenous matter. These are obtained from the food, and occur under various forms. Of all the varieties of human food, wheaten bread may be considered the type, containing more nearly than any other substance the just proportions of the several necessary principles, as shown in "The Science of Cooking Vegetarian Food."

Compare a few facts in relation to the prevailing dietetic practices of society, with those of the vegetarian system. The rearing and fattening process are very unproductive of profit to the farmer, arising from the unnatural manner in which the animals are often fed (with oil-cake, &c.), and the consequent disease and great mortality to which they are subjected. To produce 1 lb. of flesh or fat by this process, requires from 60 to 80 ozs. of oil-cake, when this is the food used, which costs the farmer from 3d. to 4d. This is to say nothing about labour, hay, &c. The wholesale price of mutton will seldom average more than 4d. or 5d. per lb., whilst experiments could be adduced to show that the cost of its production in food alone, during the process of fattening, is 6d. or 7d. per lb. The slaughtering and cooking the carcase are equally wasteful, as every operation decreases its weight, and consequent value to the consumer ; whilst, wheat, peas, beans, rice, sago, or any other farinaceous substances, which form the basis of vegetarian diet, are considerably increased in weight in their preparation as food. Thus—

12lbs of flesh will yield when cooked...................... 9lbs.
Do. of wheaten flour made into bread will yield ......16lbs.
Do. oatmeal made into porridge ....36lbs.
Do. rice stewed in water, same as oatmeal porridge...48lbs.
Do, Indian meal made into porridge, as the oatmeal 48lbs.
Do. maize powder   do...............................72lbs.
Do. hominy stewed in water, the same as oatmeal...72lbs.

See also the relative cost of various kinds of food in the table, page 17, from which we may determine what are the most economical articles of food.

Facts of this kind led PLAYFAIR to state, at an agricultural meeting at Drayton Manor, that " At London prices, a man can lay a pound of flesh upon his body with milk for 3s., with turnips for 2s. 6d., with potatoes and butcher's meat, *free from bone and fat*, for 2s., with oatmeal for 1s. 10d., with bread, flour, and barleymeal for 1s. 2d., and with beans for less than 6d. So that with an intelligent application of money we can feed four people where otherwise we can only feed one."

CHAPTER X.

MENTAL CULTURE.

MAN is a compound being. possessing animal propensities, intellectual faculties, and moral perceptions. Diet supplies the materials of which his bones, muscles, nerves, and brain are composed ; and if the brain be not the mind, it is the organ of the mind, and it must be of importance that the organ should be sound and healthy, for however skilful the musician may be, even if he could play on one string, as Paganini, he could scarcely produce superior music if that string was out of order ; but how can an instrument be other than inferior, if made of inferior materials ?—Need we wonder at this ? Can it be otherwise ? A healthy frame must form the basis for true mental culture. The first being admitted, the second must follow, as a necessary consequence : and facts prove that it is so. We might present a very long list of distinguished names and authorities, in illustration and confirmation of this view ; but will only refer to the following :—

DANIEL the prophet and his three friends, all thorough vegetarians, after a severe test by the king, " in all matters of wisdom and understanding" were *ten times* better than their competitors. See 1st chap. Daniel. Pythagoras, who laid the foundation of much of the philosophy of Greece, was a decided vegetarian ; as were also Plato (who could " reason well"), and the worthies mentioned in the last Chapter ; amongst whom we might call more especial attention to the intellectual vigor of PLUTARCH, who collected and compared the productions of the philosophers of Greece. The case of CASPER HAUSER is a very striking one, especially his power to grasp and retain every thing new to him, while a vegetarian, but which he lost, to a very considerable degree, after he became a flesh-eater. TRYON, who wrote " The way to Health, &c.," and other deeply philosophical works ; FRANKLIN, who, whilst in his youth, formed that great brain, and stored it with such amazing stores of knowledge ; SWEDENBORG, whose writings on natural philosophy, &c., consisting of some 100 volumes, written more than 100 years ago, can still be read with profit by the most advanced student ; Sir I. NEWTON, of whose intellectual greatness not a word need be said, and who, while writing his great work on Optics, lived entirely without animal food, subsisting only on bread and water ; J. WESLEY, who performed prodigies of mental and physical labor ; and HOWARD the philanthropist, the wonder of his age, who says, "I am persuaded that herbs and fruits will sustain nature in every respect, far beyond the best flesh."

The native Irish are notorious in all parts of the civilised world for their peculiar shrewdness and wit. When well educated, they are often amongst the most eloquent speakers and able writers in the world. The remarkable effect of a vegetarian diet on the intellectual powers of children was seen in the orphan asylum of Albany, N.Y., on from 80 to 130 children. Their capabilities after three years became nearly doubled. Judge Woodruff, speaking of the school of from 200 to 300 pupils, under the care of Dr. Korke at Syra, says, "These children manifested a capacity for learning which exceeded anything I had ever before or since witnessed." They were vegetarians.

THEOPHRASTES, the disciple of Plato, and who lived to the age of 107, says, "that eating much, and feeding upon flesh, makes the mind more dull, and drives it to the extreme of madness." DIOGENES attributed the dulness of the ancient Athletæ, after their departure from their original simple discipline, to their excessive use of flesh. Sir J. SINCLAIR—"Vegetable diet has a happy influence on the powers of the mind—seldom enjoyed by those who make a free use of animal food." FRANKLIN says, "It is to be preferred by those who labor with the mind." He was a living evidence of this fact. And it is notorious that of the 658 members of the House of Commons, Mr. BROTHERTON and Col. THOMPSON, both vegetarians, are able to endure the long, dreary, dull speeches better than any other members, as testified by Mr. COBDEN. LORD BYRON excluded flesh from all his meals, though his diet was not physiologically correct. SHELLEY, who has seldom been surpassed, was a strict vegetarian, and its able advocate ; his writings first drew our attention to the subject. SIR R. PHILLIPS adopted the same plan, as shown in his *Million of Facts*. DR. DICK, author of the *Christian Philosopher* and other able works, has proved what mental power can be exhibited when the dietetic habits are correct. And MILTON, whose habits were remarkably austere, chaste, and industrious, tells us "that the lyrist may indulge in wine, and a freer life, but that he who would write an epic to the nations, must eat beans and drink water." Many others might be named, did our space permit.

CHAPTER XI.

MORAL ELEVATION.

As man is the highest order of earthly beings, so his moral nature is the highest order of the man; therefore his highest mission is of a moral character. And strong as are our convictions of the advantage of a vegeterian diet, in the other respects in which we have viewed it, the moral is our favorite, and we urge the others chiefly on account of its influence on this. We would give very little to be able to bring men back to nature's simplicity, if it were only to make them better animals—though as an animal he is superior to all others—we would reform his dietetic habits, chiefly to make him better morally, that he might the better discharge his duties to God and man. We would improve his physical that he might "yield his members instruments of righteousness," to believe, love, and obey the truth, become a child of God, and an heir of a glorious immortality. Philosophy has been in the wrong, in not descending more fully into the physical man, as it is there the moral man lies concealed. For it is a well-established fact that *health* of body and mind are nearly as closely allied as the body and mind themselves— that our physical nature holds our moral nature, in a great measure, in independence—that when the habits of the animal man are bad, the moral habits cannot be good. On the other hand, when his nerves, brain, and general organic structure are in a healthy condition, the mind is beneficially and morally affected thereby, although, in many cases, we cannot tell why.

Dr. SOUTHWOOD SMITH, who has had extensive opportunities of examining the matter, asserts that filth and disease deteriorate the moral character; that the most unhealthy places produce the most immorality and the most criminals: and the Rev. C. M. TOWNSHEND, M.A., in describing his visit to the great prison of Munich, narrates a conversation he had with the governor, who said, " We find that the cooling regular diet of the prison has from the first an immense effect on the morals of the prisoners. Crime, says he, in my eyes, is a disease—a madness, and one half of the crimes on earth might be spared by a proper attention to the physical man, and to the present generation, which is to generate the next. The old Adam begets sinful children; but had the old

Adam never swerved from the diet that Providence *appointed* him, we might, at this actual time, have all of us sound stomachs, sound brains, and sound consciences." The effects of gross feeding are clearly discernable on the lower animals. The horse, by being fed on flesh, has been rendered so fierce and unmanageable as to be obliged to be kept in stalls of brass, and tied with chains of iron. Consult your lion-tamers, and the keepers of menageries ; they will tell you the same. Look also at the effect of diet on the Tartars and the Brahmins, the one as mild as the other is savage. An eminent physician, whose name we are not at liberty to mention just now, and who is one of our most popular authors, informed us not long since that "Animal food is gross feeding at the best, and is scarcely compatible with spirituality of mind, or high soaring sentiments of soul. Only those who take much exercise to work it off, to prevent it gorging and oppressing the more etherial parts of our frame, can keep clear-headed, or calm-passioned under it. I believe, says he, you could transform the most sentimental, imaginative girl into a semi-devil, by force of flesh-feeding ; and this on perfectly physiological grounds." This is strong language, but we think facts sustain and justify it.

Cruelty and crime have marked the progress of mankind, in the use of exciting meats and drinks, the one making way for the other. When Jacob brought to his father Isaac the savory meat which he loved, " he brought him wine, and he drank." Judah joined in " eating flesh and drinking wine." " Wine bibbers and riotous eaters of flesh" are not peculiar to ancient times : and we are not sure, though the apparent evils of the latter are not so great as those of the former, that they are not even more extensive ; but we do not know an argument against the use of the drink that does not apply with equal force against the flesh : and we very much question if the Temperance Reformation will be complete and permanent while flesh-eating is the general practice of its leading advocates. Animal food is undoubtedly the cause of much mischief in this respect : but we rejoice to know that some of the oldest and best friends of that good cause have discarded it with advantage to themselves and the cause they wish to promote ; and are now devoting their best energies to the cause of true, universal temperance, involving abstinence from alcohol, flesh, tobacco, tea, and coffee, with whatever else tends to set up the animal man over the intellectual and moral.

CHAPTER XII.

THE BIBLE AND SCIENCE.

WE have just read, with great delight, Sylvester Graham's *Philosophy of Sacred History*, a fit companion to his *Science of Human Life*, the former promised in the preface of the latter work. In it he has gone as fully into the Scripture bearings of the use of flesh and alcohol as he went into the Scientific in his first great work. We cannot do better than give his 181st paragraph, with one or two *verbal* omissions to save space. He says: this is "mainly a question of natural science, and as such must be solved by the revelations of God in the volume of Nature. For every law and principle and property of Nature is an institution of the Divine will—Nature being, in truth, the first great Volume of Divine Revelation, in which the deeply written will of God lies ever ready to be disclosed to the human mind by the true developments of science, and by actual experience. The Revealed Word is but a Supplement to this first great Volume, and, in strictness, as a pure revelation, contains, principally, Divine instructions concerning moral and spiritual things, which Nature speaks not of, or but faintly implies, or dimly indicates ; and hence the truth of Nature and the true meaning of the Revealed Word, must be in harmony ; and, consequently, it is impossible that the true meaning of the Revealed Word can, as a permanent law, be contrary to the laws of Nature. The truth of natural science, therefore, is the truth of God, and always comes with Divine authority to man : and the Bible, as the revealed word of God, must, when accurately interpreted, be perfectly consistent with what is true in chemistry, and mineralogy, and botany, and zoology, and astronomy, and every other natural science. Yet the Bible was not given us to teach the natural sciences ; and no correct natural philosopher thinks of going to the Bible to study these sciences. To ascertain what is true in these, he goes to the Volume of Nature as the primary and irreversible code of the omniscient and omnipotent Creator and Ruler of all things : and, in regard to his Bible, he is satisfied if he finds nothing in it, which is apparently incompatible with the demonstrations of natural science, and pleased if he finds it confirmed by scientific truth ; knowing that the truth of Nature must stand, whether the apparent meaning of any particular portion of the Sacred Scriptures agrees with it or not. He, therefore, who truly loves and reverences the Bible as the revealed word of God, will not be forward to introduce it into controversies of a scientific nature, and oppose his interpretations of it to the demonstrations of science, in such a manner as to make it appear that the Bible and the truths of natural science are at variance : for he knows that this must only serve to invalidate his Bible, and not the truth of science. But the true philosopher, who cordially and understandingly loves and reverences his Bible, will, as a scientific man, in all his investigations and researches, pursue the truth for the truth's sake ; and when he has fully ascertained the truth of science, if he finds any *apparent* want of agreement between this and his Bible, he will, with the spirit of truth still ruling his soul, honestly set about such an examination of the matter, as will enable him to show that the disagreement is only *apparent*, and that when accurately understood, the Bible perfectly harmonizes with scientific truth ; or at least, that the true meaning of the Revealed Word is not incompatible with the truth of natural science.

The truth or error of Vegetarianism is not a question of revelation, but of natural science ; as such *we* have examined it in the several preceding chapters, and must beg to say, think we have proved that the use of flesh as food cannot improve, but must deteriorate the whole complex nature of man—must multiply disease and suffering, abbreviate human life, increase the power of the animal over the intellectual and moral man, rendering him less able to understand himself, his fellow-man, or his God ; and less able and willing to understand or discharge the duties he owes to either ; and, therefore, inasmuch as he cannot attain to the highest and best state of which his nature is capable, and to which the Scriptures so earnestly exhort him, while he continues to eat flesh, the Scriptures cannot sanction his habitual use of it under ordinary circumstances.

We love the Bible as much as our objectors do—not the paper, binding, or even " the *letter* which killeth," but " the *spirit* which giveth life ;" and we are ready to sit down with any sincere believer of it, and in the light of scientific facts and demonstrations, carefully and prayerfully study it ; and believe we can show that every part of it is perfectly consistent with vegetarian doctrines.

CHAPTER XIII.

RISE AND PROGRESS OF THE VEGETARIAN SOCIETY.

WHEN important changes take place, it is natural to desire to know whence they originate, and how they were accomplished. Among the many remarkable changes of a reformatory character which have called attention to some great evil, and aroused the energies of a few to oppose them, the formation of the VEGETARIAN SOCIETY is one, which is beginning to be admitted as *a great fact.*

The Vegetarian *practice*, as we have shown, commenced by DIVINE APPOINTMENT with our first parents in the garden of Eden ; and although the practice was perhaps early broken through, no age of the world has been wholly without some noble examples of dietetic purity ; persons who, like Daniel, Pythagoras, &c., have stood forth to vindicate the honour of humanity—to demonstrate that man is capable of rising to a noble elevation—and that self-denial, benevolence, and humanity still had their residence among the inhabitants of earth.

Intemperance in eating and drinking has been the curse of all nations and ages, proving itself the most powerful incentive to all evil—the curse of the race, and especially so in Great Britain and America. A dietetic reform, therefore, was loudly called for, and Providence raised up the right sort of men to work it out, at the h ad of whom stand SYLVESTER GRAHAM in America, and JAMES SIMPSON in England ; the former, "though dead, yet speaketh." He commenced his public career as a lecturer against alcoholic drinks in the year 1830, but in 1832 devoted his main energies to the Vegetarian movement, in delivering that splendid course of lectures, since published, on the *Science of Human Life.* Mr. Simpson, who has never tasted *flesh* or *alcohol,* regarding the promotion of Vegetarianism as HIS MISSION, has, since the formation of the Society, devoted himself and his ample means with untiring zeal to its interest. DRS. MUSSEY and ALCOTT, and the REV. W. METCALFE, have, for many years, devoted themselves with great zeal to the cause in America ; and with Dr. SHEW, TRALL, NICHOLS, and others have formed a Society to work out their principles, numbering amongst its members more than 50 persons who have never tasted flesh nor alcoholic drinks.

England has had its adherents to the practice for many

years, but it was not publicly advocated as a principle till the year 1801, when the REV. W. COWHERD, of Salford, took it up, preached it from his pulpit, and established a community called "Bible Christians" on the practice. MR. GREAVES, in the year 1832, established an institution to promote its progress at Alcott House, Ham Common, Surrey, where W. OLDHAM, C. LANE, and others, did much to call attention to the subject. They established, and for some time sustained, a printing press, issuing books, tracts, and the monthly periodical called *The Healthian*, and subsequently *The New Age;* but they were before their age, and could not sustain their efforts for want of funds. In 1843 the author of this little work was convinced of the truth of Vegetarianism, by reading *Shelley*, and anxious to spread his new views, he subsequently purchased the *Truth Tester*, afterwards called the *Vegetarian Advocate*, of Dr. F. R. Lees, who was contemplating leaving this country for America. Having made it the channel of these views, a letter from a MR. WITHERS led to a conference at ALCOTT HOUSE on the 8th of. July, 1847, which resulted in another meeting, by appointment, at NORTHWOOD VILLA, Ramsgate, Kent, on the 30th Sept. following, when the VEGETARIAN SOCIETY was duly organized. Twelve of the persons present had travelled upwards of 300 miles to take part in the proceedings, some of whom had been vegetarians 35 years, and six gentlemen present were in full vigor at from 57 to 80 years of age, including J. BROTHERTON, Esq., M.P. JAMES SIMPSON, Esq., J. P., was elected President ; Mr. W. OLDHAM, Treasurer, and Mr. W. HORSELL, Secretary ; 150 names were enrolled as members.

It was a memorable occasion, which will never be forgotten by most who had the pleasure to be present.

Thus was organized an Institution, which we believe is destined to reform the dietetic habits of the whole country. It now (1856) numbers upwards of 1000 members, having local organizations in most of the chief towns, besides thousands who, though not enrolled members of the Society, are practically carrying out its principles. Many families are being trained up in these views, and a very considerable impression is made on the public mind that flesh meat is not such a valuable—indispensable—article of diet as they once thought it was. The *Vegetarian Messenger* is now the organ of the Society, while the *Journal of Health* advocates and defends its views.

44

CHAPTER XIV.

TWENTY OBJECTIONS ANSWERED.

EVERY person has a right to object, and if his objections are put in such a manner as to indicate that they are conscientious, ought to have a respectful reply; when put from a captious spirit in defence of sensual indulgence, Solomon tells us how to answer (Prov. 26, v.)

1. *God gave Noah every creeping thing for food.* Yes, and He gave the Jews "a king in his anger, and took him away in his wrath;" He also gave them flesh in the wilderness, as a punishment for their lusts; and "statutes that were not good, and judgments whereby they might not live." Ezek. xx.25.

2. *Abraham killed the fatted calf.* Yes, and so far as *intention* was concerned, he slew his son Isaac. Are you *therefore* justified in offering up your son as a burnt-offering? Many things were done—permitted—nay, commanded to be done, which were only comparatively right, even under their own circumstances.

3. *The ravens took flesh, &c. to Elijah.* Natural instincts were moved to take him flesh, but God superinduced a preternatural instinct in them to take him bread corn, or grain, as the former alone was not good for the prophet.

4. *John the Baptist ate locusts.* Yes, and Dr. FARRE speaks of an English prisoner in Algiers working, in health, 12 hours a day on bread made of the black wheat and *vegetable* locust.

5. *Peter was commanded to slay and eat.* Yes, but he refused, and yet we do not find he was punished for so doing. You ought to know that this was only a *vision*—a strong *representation* to his mind. Peter was a converted Jew, regarding the Gentiles as *unclean* persons, not within the pale of Gospel privileges; but God took this method of teaching Peter that as He had cleansed them, Peter must not call them unclean.

6. *Why were animals created?* For God's glory, man's good, and their own enjoyment. They shew the wisdom, power, and goodness as God in their organization and adaptation. They enjoy themselves most when left to their natural instincts; and in the beginning they subdued the vegetable luxuries of the earth, being the pioneers of man in subduing it; and supplying food when better was not within his reach.

7. *Flesh-eating being general, it is instinctive.* We have proved that flesh-eating is not general; and if the fact were admitted, the inference would not follow. Smoking tobacco is more general than flesh-eating; yet *nature* abhors it.

8. *I cannot live without it.* How do you know? As a proof that you have not *tried* you are alive, for if you had tried, according to your view, you would not be living to tell us you *can't* live without it. Be a *man*, and TRY IT. Begin to day.

9. *But I could not work without it.* Then you are an inferior man. We have shown you that others *can* and *do* work without it; why not you? Nearly all the hard work of the world is done by vegetarian men and animals.

10. *But what is to be done with the animals?* If you all turn Vegetarians to-morrow, turn all the animals, dogs and all, into the woods and forests, and let them shift for themselves ; or kill and bury them. You kill many *small* ones now that you do not *eat*. Do *right*, and leave the balance of creation with its Author.

11. *What are we to eat?* Any thing that your judgment approves of, besides flesh. There is an endless variety in nature, and the *Science of Cooking* will show you how to prepare them.

12. *You cannot cultivate the land.* Hand labor and machinery are more profitable than animal, and burnt turf and peat superior to animal manure or bone dust ; the former costing 8s., the latter from £4 to £7 per ton ; to say nothing of the town refuse.

13. *You cannot l've on vegetarian diet in cold climates.* The servants of the Hudson's Bay Company have proved to the contrary. They find that $2\frac{1}{2}$ lbs. of maize flour is equal, if not superior, in sustaining muscular energy, and enabling them to bear cold, to 8 lbs. of fat meat, which constitutes the usual allowance. *Iceland moss*, the food of the reindeer, is very nutritious, and MOST ABUNDANT in Lapland, even in *mid*-winter.

14. *What will you do for shoes, soap, and candles?* Manufacture them of vegetable products, which nature and art are supplying as fast as demands are being made upon them. "Necessity is the mother of invention ;" already we have several.

15. *You kill more animals than we do.* How? *In your water vegetables, fruits, &c.* We deny this, and call on you to *prove* it. True, *impure* water, and *decayed* vegetables, &c., "contain myriads of living animals," but we reject all such as food.

16. *Yours are new fangled notions.* Many new things are good, and none are bad *because* they are *new*, as steam power, gas, &c. Vegetarianism began with the creation of man, and never ceased.

17. *You are a set of enthusiasts.* It is much more easy to call hard names than to answer hard arguments, and put down hard facts. What does an enthusiast mean? *A man in earnest—* "zealously affected in a good thing;" a *living* man who can go against the stream—who dares to be singular, and to suffer.

18. *You are all crazy.* So *you* say, but others do not. So you *say*, but we are not sure you *think* so. Perhaps some people say the same of you. Men are not generally good for much till the world pronounce them crazy. Felix said Paul was mad.

19. *Paul said in the latter day some would depart from the faith, forbid to marry,* and command to abstain from meats, &c. Vegetarians do not forbid to marry ; they themselves marry ; they do not *command* to abstain from meats, they only *advise*. But you do not eat cats, toads, &c., though "creatures of God."

20. *I like it, and will have it.* This is *honest*, but so says the washerwoman of her gin, and is no argument in its favour. Still it is a *settler*, for who ever thinks of *reasoning* with a man when he puts himself under PRINCE PALATF, who is self-willed and unreasonable, having neither eyes nor ears.

TWELVE REASONS FOR NOT EATING FLESH.

1.—Because anatomy and physiology prove that the whole nature of man is more appropriately adapted to a vegetarian, than to a flesh diet.

2.—Because in the earliest dietetic table extant, no mention is made of the flesh of animals. It is as follows:—"God said, behold I have given you every herb bearing seed which is upon the face of all the earth, and every tree in the which is the fruit of a tree yielding seed, to you it shall be for meat." Gen. i. 29.

3.—Because God's word and our nature say *Thou shalt not kill;* and unless we kill animals, or employ others to do it, we cannot procure flesh for food.

4.—Because the blood is the life of man, therefore the purer the blood, the healthier the man. And all facts prove that blood made from vegetarian food is purer than that made from a mixed diet.

5.—Because every constituent of the body of man and animals, is derived from plants, and not a single element is generated by the vital principle,—man and animals, therefore, only appropriating the already formed organized productions of vegetable matter.

6.—Because it follows from the former fact, that those who partake of the flesh of animals as food, can obtain no additional element in such food, capable of forming purer blood; on the contrary, they risk the introduction into their system of the elements of various diseases with which the animals might have been infected.

7.—Because a vegetarian diet will sustain a man in perfect health at a much less cost than a mixed diet.

8.—Because feeding animals for the purpose of killing them and eating their flesh, is a circuitous and expensive way of obtaining food.

9.—Because partaking of the flesh of animals as food, gives an undue stimulus to the propensities, which frequently goad individuals on to the commission of offences against the moral laws of God and man.

10.—Because the long experience of numerous persons in most parts of the world, on vegetarian diet, enabling some of them to endure more than ordinary physical and mental labour, in almost uninterrupted good health, are "stubborn facts."

11.—Because, since it is an admitted fact among most intellectual men, that the body of man is the organism through which the soul makes manifest its wants and purposes in this life, that great physical energy, and high intellectual attainments, and moral purity, are incompatible with gross and diseased organism; therefore a vegetarian diet is more favourable to health of body and mind than one of flesh.

12.—Because the chemical analysis of Liebig, Playfair, and other *modern* chemists prove that peas, beans, lentiles, and wheat, contain more per cent. of the element of nutriment, than beef and other kinds of flesh.